FARM-FRESH CATS

by SCOTT SANTORO

HarperCollins*Publishers*

Library of Congress Cataloging-in-Publication Data
Santoro, Scott.   Farm-fresh cats / by Scott Santoro. — 1st ed.   p.   cm.
Summary: A farmer is surprised to discover that he has grown a crop
of very unusual cats instead of cabbages.
ISBN-10: 0-06-078178-5 (trade bdg.) — ISBN-13: 978-0-06-078178-1 (trade bdg.)
ISBN-10: 0-06-078179-3 (lib. bdg.) — ISBN-13: 978-0-06-078179-8 (lib. bdg.)
[1. Cats—Fiction. 2. Farm life—Fiction.] I. Title.
PZ7.S23855Far 2006   [E]—dc22   2005014511 CIP   AC

Typography by Carla Weise
1 2 3 4 5 6 7 8 9 10
❖
First Edition

3 9082 10220 4784

In memory of my grandparents
Ray and Norma Wolfe

Farmer Ray was an ordinary man.
Norma was his ordinary wife.

Farmer Ray loved all
the animals on his farm.

So did Norma.

And all the animals loved them.
It was a very happy and ordinary little farm.

But one night something happened.

No one ever found out exactly what it was, but everyone agreed that it must have been something extraordinary.

The next morning
Farmer Ray was
eager to
check on his
cabbage crop.

He got a big surprise.

Farmer Ray noticed right away that
instead of nice green cabbage heads,
there were nice green CAT heads
peeking out of the ground. They looked
at him with their strange orange eyes.

"Why, that's funny," said Farmer Ray.
"I was sure I planted cabbages."

He brought Norma
out to show her.

"How very odd," she said.
"I've never seen green cats before."
They agreed, however, that the cats
were a very nice crop.

A few weeks later the cats were mewing at Farmer Ray,
and it seemed to him that they wanted to be picked.

Though it was hard to tell which ones were ripe, Farmer Ray and Norma picked some and took them to the house.

Some were picked
too early.

Some were picked
too late.

The regular cats were
suspicious of them
from the start.

Their litter box became a flower garden,
which Norma found charming.
"Why, these cats are no more trouble
than houseplants," she said happily.

They didn't even
chase mice.

"They do shed," said Farmer Ray, "and I think there are more of them every day."

Every fur ball that rolled under the television
or lodged between the sofa cushions
sprouted a new cat.

In just a few weeks there were hundreds
and hundreds of them—on the rooftops,
in the cellar, in the barn, in the trees.

They were EVERYWHERE!

The other animals threatened to leave unless something was done. Farmer Ray was worried. "What shall we do?" he asked. "We have more cats than we have vegetables."

"I have an idea," said Norma.

The city people who usually stopped at Farmer Ray and Norma's stand to buy vegetables were all very busy. They loved the idea of having pets that were no more trouble than potted plants. Soon they called all their busy friends on their cell phones. As quickly as all those city people arrived, the cats were all gone.

Farmer Ray and Norma had a lovely picnic on the lawn.
The happy little farm was no longer extraordinary,
and all the animals were happy again.

That night Farmer Ray and Norma
looked up at the sky and thought
that, just for a moment, the man
in the moon looked like a cat.

"I don't think we've seen
the last of them,"
whispered Farmer Ray.

What do **YOU** think?